TIMELESS TALES
FROM THE SUMMER LANDS

*An illustrated collection of Cornish stories
in verse, revised and updated*

Verses - TONY COTTRELL

Artwork - BARRY COTTRELL

drivenLine

MMXXII

First published by Panacea Press, Polruan, Cornwall in 1993 as *Tales from the Summer Lands: A Collection of Cornish Stories in Verse*

This edition published by drivenLine in 2022 as *Timeless Tales from the Summer Lands: An illustrated collection of Cornish stories in verse, revised and updated* with a catalogue list of the linocut illustrations

drivenLine
The Clock House
Widford
Burford
OX18 4DU
United Kingdom
www.drivenline.uk

Two earlier revised and updated limited editions of this book were published in 2015 by Panacea Press under the title *More Tales from the Summerlands: A Second Collection of Cornish Stories in Verse (author's edition and artist's edition)* with essentially the same content as this edition

ISBN: 978-1-7399205-5-5

The front cover image is *Morveren*, linocut, from 'The Mermaid of Zennor' in this collection

Designed by Barry Cottrell
www.barrycottrell.com
Printed by Ingram Content Group UK Ltd

CONTENTS *(with locations and settings)*

"…she ran free most joyously"

Cornwall is almost an island, surrounded on three sides by the sea and, to the East, virtually cut off from England by the River Tamar. This is the legend of the birth of that river

THE SOURCE OF THE TAMAR

Tamara was an erstwhile sprite
Before Man had invented Time,
The daughter of two troglodites
Who found their darkened cave sublime.
Within the earth they shunned the light
And would not share their child's delight
As she ran free
Most joyously
Across the moor towards the sea.

Soon upon these carefree outings
She was joined by two young giants;
Taw and Tavy, where her pouting
Lips and eyes that sparked defiance
Had the giants' love-buds sprouting,
Had them self-penned sonnets spouting
While she ran free
Most joyously
Across the moor towards the sea.

Both the love-struck boobies doted
On Tamara to distraction;
Begged that one of them be voted
Favourite but her reaction
Was to say - and here I've quoted -
"Both of you should be devoted
While I run free
Most joyously
Across the moor towards the sea."

Just then, this 'tête à tête à tête'
Was interrupted by her father
Who claimed she'd stayed out far too late
But Tamara said she'd rather
Stay some more, she'd come to hate
Their dreary cave - up here was great -
Where she ran free
Most joyously
Across the moor towards the sea.

At this her father gave a yell
Directing it at Taw and Tavy,
Cast a universal spell,
Put them to sleep and with a wave, he
Turned Tamara in that dell
Into a stream that burbling fell
And then ran free
Most joyously
Across the moor towards the sea.

The giants woke, and ran home screaming,
Where poor Tavy's warlock father
Realised there's no redeeming
Tavy from his love-lorn lather.
So he satisfied his dream and
Turned his son into the stream
That then ran free
Most joyously
Across the moor
And joined Tamara
Thence together to the sea.

Tamara is turned into a stream

What, though, was poor Taw's position,
In despair for his lost lover?
He too sought a wise magician
Who transformed him, like the other.
Once again a liquid lover
Flowed in search of intersection
But too late, poor Taw discovered
He flowed in the wrong direction!
While they ran free
Most joyously
Across the moor towards the sea -
Though near their source,
Apart their mouths;
North lay *his* course
While theirs ran south!

The Giant's Hedge

THE GIANT'S HEDGE

One day, a giant with nothing to do
Planted a hedge from Lerryn to Looe.
Straight across meadows, through streams and round woods,
There now was this hedge where once nothing had stood.
To call it a hedge although, wasn't quite right -
It was more of a ditch seen in some sort of light -
Even that wasn't it, more a hybrid or cross,
A rampart or moat, no - the word is a 'fosse.'
It was made out of earth and then planted with trees -
For a giant, a most unaccountable wheeze.
When asked why he did it, the giant said: "I'm
Not sure - it was something to help pass the time."

SAINTS AND SINNERS

In Cornwall we're not short
Of Tres and Pols and Ports
Of villages both picturesque and quaint;
But of one thing you will count
An inordinate amount
And that's obscure and curious Celtic saints.

There's St. Erney and St. Ewe,
St. Issy and St. Kew,
Sts. Ildierna, Petroc and St. Ives,
St. Goran and St. Gwithian,
St. Stithney and St. Stithian,
But not a lot is known about their lives.

So rather than compile
Just an alphabetic file
Of these doughty folk from Ireland, France and Wales,
I'll attempt to realise
Some of them, before your eyes
By telling you a couple of their tales.

Now the hardest task they faced,
Trying to pros'lytize the place,
Was a deep-engrained old Celtic predilection:
The Cornish chiefs, it's said,
Would chop off all strangers' heads,
Which proved to be a real indisposition.

Yes, Tewdrig was the name
Of the chief whose greatest fame
Was this rather drastic cure for propagation.
He was active just by Hayle
Where the mission'ries, whole-sale,
Were rounded up for swift decapitation.

But obviously it's true
That some of them got through
And even those who died have been remembered;
St. Gwinear for one
With whom Tewdrig had his fun
But he's still been sanctified for being dismembered.

"...a real indisposition..."

At least St. Columb landed;
But then she could not stand the
Unwanted propositions of a suitor.
But the man would not take 'no'
For poor Columb's answer, so
As he couldn't have her love, he'd execute her.

And it wasn't just the males
But the supposedly more frail
And weaker sex who also plagued the holy.
For an Englishman, St. Cleer,
Had set up shop down here
In a hermitage both solit'ry and lowly.

But the trouble was, this preacher
Was a rather handsome creature
Who made a more than spiritual impression
And among those who'd been smitten
Was the local lady chieftain
Who wanted Cleer for individual sessions.

So St. Cleer tried a rebuff -
He was above that sort of stuff,
His thoughts lay higher than such carnal deeds.
But the chieftainess said: "No, mate!
All that higher stuff can wait -
I want to satisfy more basic needs!"

But Cleer would not transgress
And was forced to flee, no less;
He went to France to try to 'scape this doxy.
But the lady was a tartar,
Insisted no man would outsmart her
And had St. Cleer beheaded there, by proxy.

Yes, the Cornish saints are legion -
They reached all parts of the region

"...the lady was a tartar"

Where they spread a mix of gospel and sedition;
But if you'd like some more
Of this saintly Celtic lore,
You'll have to wait until the next edition.

St Cleer was rather handsome

ENTERPRISE AND INITIATIVE

Zephania Job

Polperro men, like all of their neighbours,
Augmented their income with clandestine labours;
They would sail 'cross the Channel on this task you understand
And the fruit of their toils was contraband.

Yes, all this work was a sign of ambition -
Indeed, those free traders seemed to start a tradition,
For those smugglers established a business of their own
In what you might call the first enterprise zone.

Now Zephania Job was the Polperro teacher;
Perhaps not an overtly prominent creature,
But Zephania's gift to the place was paramount
'Cos he taught all the children to count.

See, it's all very well getting hold of the booty
And landing it thereby avoiding the duty,
But you need to keep a record of the various amounts
And someone who can convert cost in francs to cost in pounds!

So if the little children, too small to carry plunder,
Can tally up the total without making a blunder
And multiply the dividends and then divide the takings,
You've got a young accountant there, a merchant in the makings.

And when the totals mounted high and looked like going higher,
The traders of Polperro simply called on Zephania
Who to their business proposition quickly did consent
And charged on ev'ry load a dividend of one per cent.

Now one per cent (plus postage) may not sound like a mint
But very soon it all adds up, and Zephania wasn't skint.
By each percent he rose another notch, another rank,
He made so much he even had to open his own bank.

He invested it in limekilns, in Polperro cutters,
He made the people prosperous and raised them from the gutter,
And when in Eighteen Twenty Two he finally was took,
He died safe in the knowledge that they'd all got balanced books.

Yes, Zephania Job was the Polperro teacher
Who ensured that Polperro had this outstanding feature:
The children all could do their sums, could add and multiply
And help support their fathers in their private enterprise.

LOCAL LOVE STORY

It was by the Fowey river that Tristan and Yseut,

Their love enmeshed with hurt, played out their tragic drama.

In epic verse, to music, you've heard the classic story

Of chivalry and glory, love-potions and betrayal,

But truthfully this epic has sources more prosaic

Than a mythical mosaic of knights in shining armour.

Along bridlepaths and hedgerows, and not from hist'ry's pages,

A light from down the ages shows a more ordin'ry portrayal.

In the parish of St. Samson beside the Fowey's waters,

King Mark made his headquarters, at Castle Dore his fort.

His palace was in Lantyan but this was not a mansion,

No fanciful expansion, just a stockade and a hall.

No fairy tale confection, but the best-placed situation

That gave fortification to the king and to his court.

Fresh water, food and shelter, with Castle Dore's asylum -

A well-defended island, here Mark had found it all.

And in this world of wattle, of earth and wood and water,
The King of Ireland's daughter arrived at Tristan's side.
The nephew of the ruler already'd proved his brav'ry,
Had saved the king from slav'ry by fighting for his name.
Yes, Tristan fought the Morholt,
Who had challenged Cornwall's finest,
He had killed the Irish tyrant in the river at low tide
And then set off to Ireland to find King Mark a consort
From whence he had to transport this strange lady back again.

And on the homeward journey across the Irish ocean,
By chance they shared a potion which was mutually seducing.
The details of their drama are elsewhere well related,
Their constancy narrated, their deceptions and their flight;
Of how they fled to Truro to the forest near to Malpas
And there devoid of help as their few scant supplies reducing,
They sought to find forgiveness by a return to obligations,
But the dread predestination could not free them from their plight.

Tristan and Yseut

They tried to do their duty but a more basic force was stronger,
It wasn't right or wrong or chivalry that ruled their lives:
It was destiny that held them, ill-luck that had dominion -
It's a matter of opinion if such forces still hold sway.
But no matter what the motive, you cannot escape the setting
And it's even more befitting when it's there before your eyes -
You walk through the woods round Fowey
In the moonlight or the mist and
You know Yseut and Tristan are not far away today.

…not far away today

THE DEATH OF THE GIANT BOLSTER

Bolster was a Cornish giant
Quite colossal, although pliant -
His left foot stood upon Carn Brea,
His right on cliffs six miles away!
Bolster, although huge was gentle,
Verging on the sentimental;
He loved St. Agnes, who was vexed
Because she'd vowed to give up sex.
And anyway, the thought of 'action'
With poor Bolster lacked attraction
Because, if I'm to be quite frank,
Poor Bolster very simply stank!
This nescience of deodorants
Meant Bolster did not stand a chance
But rather than inform him that
A whiff of him just knocked her flat,
Instead of giving it him straight
St. Agnes planned an awful fate.
(Indeed, her actions were not faintly
What I'd epitomize as saintly!)

Bolster – a pliant giant

She showed the poor besotted sap
Apparently a little gap,
Said: "Just to prove your love's not dud
Please fill this hole up with your blood.
Compared to you, it's very small
It shouldn't trouble you at all!"
As I've already said, this giant
Although colossal was so pliant
That, not suspecting any harm,
He stuck his knife into his arm.
Ignoring any sense of pain,
He opened wide the massive vein
And let his blood gush from above
In an attempt to please his love.

But the sanctimonious bitch
Had kept from him the one fact which
Was that the hole - yes, you can guess -
In fact was really bottomless.
A cave beneath the cranny gave
Eternal access to the waves -
No matter how much Bolster bled
The fissure never filled - instead,
Too weak to see where it was leading,
The doting fool just kept on bleeding.

He tried to answer his beloved
But fainted before he discovered
That his token of affection -
This trusting act of self-dissection -
Was not a silly lover's whim
But rather to get rid of him.

And bleeding on, poor Bolster died,
His life blood ebbing with the tide.

But Agnes didn't 'scape scot free
For, where the blood flowed to the sea,
There where poor Bolster's blood ran forth
Which people now call Chapel Porth,
In mem'ry of the poor duped dead
The very rocks remain bright red;
A witness, for eternity,
Of woman's harsh duplicity.

And that is how poor Bolster died
In an attempt to win a bride.
The moral learned from that day hence:
It isn't wise to fancy saints.

"*He...let his blood gush*"

Tin was the backbone of the Cornish economy for thousands of years but, in a Christian society, the legend of its discovery was ascribed to the patron saint

THE DISCOVERY OF TIN

St. Piran was an Irish priest
Who was not popular; - at least
His parish showed its views this way -
By dumping him in Dublin Bay.
And lest it seem too esoteric -
This verdict on their erstwhile cleric -
To emphasise their true respect,
They tied a millstone round his neck.
But strange to say, he did not drown;
The millstone kept him up, not down;
Though not a customary boat
The millstone kept our man afloat.
And borne by the prevailing flow
He came to Perranzabuloe.
(Of course, it wasn't called that then -
They named it later, after him -
It must have had a diff'rent name
But after, with its claim to fame,
They changed it, did St. Piran's fans,
It means: 'St. Piran in the Sands'.)

"The millstone kept our man afloat"

He got there somehow, still 'extant',
The latest Irish immigrant
And just to prove it was no joke
He set about converting folk.

But where the life of Piran varies
From that of other missionaries
Was in the way he found, by chance,
A very happy circumstance.

One day as he was going to cook
His breakfast, chose as inglenook
A flat, black stone which, it transpired,
Was perfect for his cooking fire.
But as the fire grew nice and hot
He saw, beneath his cooking pot,
A stream of bright white metal ran
From out the rock onto the sand.
Yes - that was Cornwall's wealth's beginning -
St. Piran had discovered tinning!

"Piran fancying something hot"

That industry was the upshot
Of Piran fancying something hot.
And to remind us of his find
The Cornish flag has been designed -
Two simple themes you find therein,
The black of stone, the white of tin,
The white cross on the black background
Commemorates how tin was found.

The Cornish Flag

BARKER'S KNEE

The knockers live in tin mines,
A race as old as time;
Before the Celt invasion
Was the ancient knockers' prime.
They were not fit for Heaven,
Nor bad enough for Hell,
And so they chose the tin mines
As the place in which to dwell.

Now, knockers, for the most part,
Are loath to interfere -
They are not ostentatious
And don't like to appear.
The miners often hear them
At work along the seam
But to try by choice to see them
Is a very silly scheme.

Young Barker was a tinner -
A lazy, doubting chap -
He had no faith in knockers,
Said it was just claptrap.
His mates told him: "Be careful!
It isn't wise to scoff."
But Barker said: "You prove it me -
Until then, bugger off!"

His mates said he was silly,
The knockers could be cruel
They had their sense of justice,
He'd best not play the fool.
But Barker would not listen,
He said: "I'll tell you what,
I'll prove there's no such nonsense,
Today, as like it not!"

He lay down at the pit head
Although he thought it daft
To listen for the knockers
At work down in the shaft.
At first it all was silence
But then he caught the drift
Of shrill, inhuman voices
As they stopped their eight-hour shift.

They didn't seem to notice
The presence of the spy
So Barker tried to watch them
By means of naked eye.
He edged a little closer,
Contrived to take a peek -
They looked like wizened children
With wrinkled, leathern cheeks.

He placed his pickaxe on Barker's knee

They all were busy hiding
Their mining impliments;
One hid his in a rock cleft
Another in a vent.
"And I shall place my pickaxe,"
Cried one triumphantly -
"To make the most impression -
And that's on - Barker's knee!"

They turned to face poor Barker
Who stared incred'lously.
They screamed and crowded as, unseen,
A weight smashed his right knee.
He never told what happened there,
No, nothing would he say,
But Barker limped and hobbled from
Then, till his dying day.

"...Old Nick stays forth"

THE ROUND HOUSES OF VERYAN

Veryan folk are on the level -
Will not entertain the Devil
And to ensure Old Nick stays forth,
They won't have doors that face the North.
And to guarantee Old Scratch
Cannot abide beneath their thatch,
Not one dark corner can be found -
The Veryan houses' walls are round!

THE BALLAD OF JAN TREGEAGLE

I'll tell you the tale of Jan Tregeagle -
Oh, his soul it was black for his life it was evil!
Ev'ry species of sin had besmirched his life,
He had strangled his children and murdered his wife.

He then set about seducing rich ladies,
Inheriting their wealth before sending them to Hades,
Stealing estates from orphans by swindling
And selling his soul once his assets were dwindling.

A pact with the Devil, they supposed he'd made,
But of Hell's damnation he didn't seem afraid.
For when he died they still laid him in holy ground
For he'd paid for his grave with many a pound.

But his ill-bought bed was no resting place:
'Twas Assises day, they were trying a case -
A large sum of money had been lent way back
With Jan the only witness to the so-called pact.

The debtor was a braggart, a fool also;
He couldn't let enough alone, he just had to crow:
"If Jan do say I 'ad the sum, come tell it to my face!
I call forth Tregeagle from 'is resting place!"

The court then went cold at the name of the dead;
People crossed themselves and they bowed their heads.
For in walked black Jan from his grave nearby
To the witness box, there to testify.

"In my life, my name was Jan Tregeagle -
This idiot is in the wrong - the plaintiff's case is legal!
Is this the only reason, this petty, trifling test,
That now Old Nick can take me as I'm called from my last rest?"

The Clergy then was summoned for they felt duty bound
To save the poor soul from the black hell hounds
For the waking dead called forth from the grave
Must work for Eternity, their souls for to save.

"...the Devil and his dogs"

So they set him to empty the dark Dozmary pool
Armed just with a limpet shell, a hellish choice of tool,
A limpet shell with holes in - a hopeless, hapless task -
But it kept him from the hounds of Hell,
Which was all that he could ask.

Through the long black nights he worked the world away;
He had to work eternally to keep the pack at bay;
Then one fell night with the storms round his head,
He left his toil and 'cross the moor he fled.

And hard at his heels, the Devil and his dogs
Chasing Jan to the safety of the cross.
'Cross the moors to the church that stands on Roche rock
And he banged on the doors but the door it was locked!

His head was inside so they couldn't take his soul
But the screams of poor Jan set the rocks to roll
Till the priest of the rock couldn't stand no more,
And he sent poor Jan down to work on the shore.

To work on the shore weaving sand into ropes -
A task so hard as to destroy all life's hopes;
But he worked on the shore down beside Padstow -
And the sea washed his work when the tide 'gan to flow.

"...his screams you can hear"

And the howls of frustration from poor sad Jan
Could be heard as the tide washed away the sand
Till a saint that was by a sand rope did bend
Then drove Jan west till he came to Land's End.

And it's there that he toils to this very day,
Sweeping the sand from Porthcurno Bay;
He is still at his task and his screams you can hear,
Howling above the gales quite clear;
For the Atlantic sea always throws back the sand
So his task never ends and his soul stays undamned.

"A limpet shell with holes in"

PISKIES

It's only in the last few years,
No more than, say, two hundred,
That precious folk would say: It's risky
Not to call a sprite a 'pisky'
When you're down in Cornwall.
Up till then - 'pixie' would do;
But if you're being picky
The piskies came in many guises
Many likenesses and sizes,
Boggarts, bucas, bucaboo,
All wicked types of goblin who
Are ill-disposed, unkind to man-
They nip and pinch them when they can.

There's knockers from deep in the mines
They dupe and hoodwink those they find
Who've strayed beyond where they should be-
You'll find some more in 'Barker's Knee'.

"...spriggans are those best avoided"

But spriggans are those best avoided,
For once those wee folk were employed, they'd
Lead the lost through barren places,
Over cliffs and then their faces
As a rule dire as can be
Would take on grimaces of glee!

"St Cury had a wondrous fish"

ST CURY'S FISH

Saint Cury had a wondrous fish
Which fed him in his cell;
He'd cut a slice off ev'ry night-
Next morning it was well.
However much the saint would eat
Would grow back by the morn;
The fish was there, and as complete
As the day on which 'twas born.
St Cury praised this miracle
To God with heart and voice;
But wonder, would he not have liked
A little bit of choice?

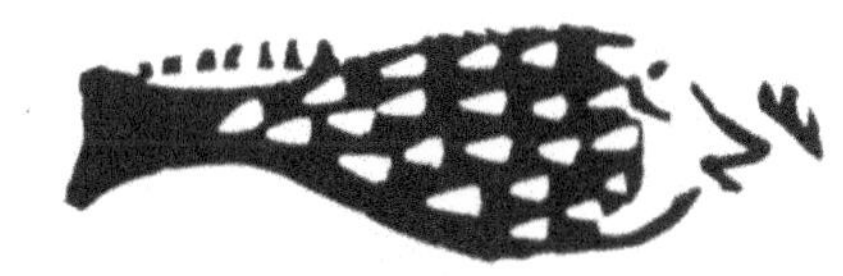

LEAVING BY LEAF

Ia was a young coleen
Who planned to spread the word,
She was pious, she was keen
But an accident occurred:
Instead of sailing off to sea
The others left her on the quay;
They wouldn't let her on the ship;
She was too young to make the trip.

She sat upon the shore and cried;
Quite dreadful was her grief
She prayed to God and then espied
A rather buoyant leaf.
She found nearby a sort of rod
And gave the leaf a sort of prod
And watched as there before her eyes
The leaf swelled to a whopping size.

"She steered for foreign parts"

This obviously was sent from God
So without any charts
And with the aid of that same rod
She steered for foreign parts.
Cornwall was the destination
For her chosen ministration.
But her ardour soon abated -
Poor Ia was decapitated!

THE MERMAID OF ZENNOR

Zennor clings to the northern cliff,
A few miles away from Land's End
The waves can be wild and the breezes be stiff
And the sea be both foeman and friend.

The church of Senara, a Britanny saint,
Commands what there is of a view,
Not a great beauty but certainly quaint
And famed for the end of one pew.
For there a crude, almost childish design
Draws people from throughout the land-
The mermaid of Zennor, almost a shrine
To what once took place, close at hand:

Mathew Trevella was a fine handsome lad,
Sang solos in the church choir;
And people who heard him were no longer sad,
His singing would cheer and inspire.

And out of the church door and over the quay
This glorious voice could be heard;
Thence over the waves, even under the sea
Each sensitive spirit was stirred.

"The greatest gift to Man on earth-
The wondrous trinity,
Inherited at ev'ry birth:
The air, the land and sea.

So let us recognise we're kin
On air and land and sea
To ev'ry soul that dwells therein
And live in harmony."

So Mathew would sing of a clear Sunday night
His voice ringing out, fine and strong
While far out to sea, someone, out of sight,
Had also been touched by his song.

"*Mathew's voice rang out*"

Morveren

Morveren, the mermaid, the daughter of Llyr
The king of the world 'neath the sea,
Was wholly enraptured by what she could hear
And had to know what it could be.

Nearer each Sunday she'd swim on the tide
The higher, the nearer her perch;
Spellbound by what she could hear from inside
Radiating from the church.

Till one night the singing had given her strength
To hobble and stumble ashore
And stand in the shadow there until, at length
Mathew looked up to the door.

He saw this fantastical, beautiful maid
With coral and pearls in her hair
As if, from his fancy an angel had strayed
And charmingly was standing there.

"Don't go" he cried out but she said for her part:
"I have to flee, I cannot stay.
I belong to the sea, though you've captured my heart,
I would perish before break of day."

"Then I shall go with you," and he picked up the maid
Who cried: "Take me back to the sea."
So into the high tide he started to wade
Till they both were submerged, gradually.

The village had lost a good, honest son
Although, if we're truthful, not quite -
For, for those who would listen, his songs linger on
As he sings to his bride, in the night.

Not just songs of love; also songs of the sea
Which fortell what King Llyr would do;
His songs told the fisherfolk how it would be,
And more often than not, they'd be true.

The wind and the waves would caution the men
Whether to fish or stay home
And Mathew's fine tenor would echo again
From far out to sea, 'cross the foam.

"From far out to sea, 'cross the foam"

Parson Troutbeck

PARSON TROUTBECK

Parson Troutbeck lived on Scilly
Unremarkably until he
Voiced the famous observation
On the subject of salvation.
Not the saving of transgressors
But of salvage from wrecked vessels.
Saying: "Lord, we don't importune
That Thou visit the misfortune
Of wrecking on ships by intention
But if, despite Thine intervention,
This should come to pass, we pray
That Thou wilt guide the wrecks our way."

And later, into church one morning
Someone rushed to shout a warning
That a wreck had just been sighted
But before his flock took flight, the
Parson called to lock the portal,
'Gan to preach that their immortal
Souls they'd lose if the'd not heed
His warnings on the sin of Greed.

And as he preached, he paced the floor
And strode towards the church's door.
"Let no man rush to search for plunder!"
So saying, pushed the doors asunder.

"Or if we must," - and here's the sequel -
"At least let each man start off equal!"
This said, and with no further check,
He led the race down to the wreck.

"He led the race down to the wreck."

LYONNESSE

Out to the West, beyond Land's End
Between here and the Scilly Isles
Across a space of thirty miles
Undying ancient tales extend
Of sunken towns and sumptuousness,
The long-lost land of Lyonnesse.

It spread for thirty miles or more;
A thriving country full of folk
Who lived and loved 'till, at a stroke,
One fateful day, across the shore
The sea proved her possessiveness
And inundated Lyonnesse.

And, like a man dead in his prime,
The myths and legends soon took hold:

How Lyonnesse was built in gold
And slumb'ring, would awake in time;
How church bells tolled beneath the sea
And Scilly was its cemet'ry.

"How church bells tolled beneath the sea"

Indeed the scholars now have said
The Scilly archipelago
Was mountains which the folk below
Would climb and there inter their dead.
So when the flood forced men to yield,
It left us this Elysian field.

And standing now on Gwennap Head,
You face the fading, ev'ning heat,
It is no vast fantastic feat
To conjure islands of the dead:
See Tristan's home, where he has gone,
And Arthur's final Avalon.

"And standing now on Gwennap Head"

Catalogue list of illustrations

All artwork was made using the printmaking technique of linocut.
The lino blocks were originally printed by hand on buff-coloured
Japanese *bunkoshi* 70gsm paper.

<table>
<tr><td>THE SOURCE OF THE TAMAR</td><td></td><td>Image</td><td>Paper</td></tr>
<tr><td>p.4   "...she ran free, most joyously"</td><td>*</td><td>11.7. x 9.0</td><td>21.0 x 16.0</td></tr>
<tr><td>p.8   Tamara is turned into a stream</td><td>*</td><td>16.5 x 12.0</td><td>22.2 x 18.0</td></tr>
<tr><td>THE GIANT'S HEDGE</td><td></td><td></td><td></td></tr>
<tr><td>p.10 The Giant's Hedge</td><td></td><td>5.5 x 10.2</td><td>10.5 x 16.0</td></tr>
<tr><td>SAINTS AND SINNERS</td><td></td><td></td><td></td></tr>
<tr><td>p.14 "...a real indisposition..."</td><td></td><td>10.0 x 12.0</td><td>17.5 x 22.5</td></tr>
<tr><td>p.16 "...the lady was a tartar"</td><td>*</td><td>9.0 x 4.5</td><td>15.0 x 10.0</td></tr>
<tr><td>p.17 St Cleer was rather handsome</td><td>*</td><td>12.2 x 5.7</td><td>16.5 x 10.8</td></tr>
<tr><td>ENTERPRISE AND INITIATIVE</td><td></td><td></td><td></td></tr>
<tr><td>p.18 Zephania Job</td><td></td><td>5.6 x 7.5</td><td>11.0 x 12.1</td></tr>
<tr><td>LOCAL LOVE STORY</td><td></td><td></td><td></td></tr>
<tr><td>p.23 Tristan and Yseut</td><td>*</td><td>12.0 x 9.2</td><td>21.0 x 16.7</td></tr>
<tr><td>p.24 "...not far away today"</td><td></td><td>detail from p. 23</td><td></td></tr>
</table>

Catalogue list of illustrations

The sizes are shown in centimetres of the original block prints and the paper they were printed on, before being digitally resized and printed in black-and-white for this book.

		Image	Paper
DEATH OF THE GIANT BOLSTER			
p.26	*Bolster – a pliant giant*	*17.7 x 12.5*	*25.5 x 19.5*
p.29	*"He...let his blood gush"*	*11.8 x 9.3*	*21.0 x 16.7*
THE DISCOVERY OF TIN			
p.31	*"The millstone kept our man afloat" **	*7.5 x 12.0*	*16.0 x 22.0*
p.33	*"Piran fancying something hot"*	*11.6 x 8.0*	*21.3.x 16.5*
BARKER'S KNEE			
p.38	*He placed his pickaxe ...*	*12.0 x 11.5*	*22.0. x 17.7*
THE ROUND HOUSES OF VERYAN			
p.40	*"...Old Nick stays forth"*	** 12.0 x 10.0*	*21.0 x 17.0*
THE BALLAD OF JAN TREGEAGLE			
p.44	*"...the devil and his dogs"*	** 11.6 x 14.7*	*17.5 x 22.0*
p.46	*"...his screams you can hear ..."*	** 13.5 x 12.0*	*22.0 x 17.5*

Catalogue list of illustrations

Illustrations available for sale – marked with an asterisk * – are
printed by hand to order, in limited editions of 50, except for
Morveren, printed in a limited edition of 250.

		Image	Paper
PISKIES			
p.49 "…spriggans are those best avoided"		15.0 x 20.0	22.0 x 26.0
ST CURY'S FISH			
p.50 "St Cury had a wondrous fish"	*	19.0 x 14.1	29 x 21.5
LEAVING BY LEAF			
p.53. "…She steered for foreign parts"	*	11.2 x 10.0	21.0 x 16.5
THE MERMAID OF ZENNOR			
p.57 Mathew's voice rang out		11.8 x 9.0	21.0 x 16.5
p.58 Morveren	*	10.2 x 5.3	17.5 x 9.0
p.61 "From far out to sea, 'cross the foam"		detail from p.57	
PARSON TROUTBECK			
p.62 Parson Troutbeck		11.1 x 9.0	21.0 x 17.0
p.65 "…He led the race down to the wreck"		4.0 x 9.3 (max.)	10.0 x 16.0
LYONNESSE			
p.67 "…To conjure islands of the dead"	*	8.4 x 12.5	17.3 z 22.0
p.69 "…standing now on Gwennap Head" *		12.0 x 9.5	21.0 x 17.0

[73]

Tony's verse is set in the semi-mythical realm of the Summer Lands to the far southwest of England. Cornwall is unique in being a clearly bounded land still steeped in legend. Here, the veil between the worlds is thin, and while the 'Summer Lands,' may suggest for some the peaceful Otherworld of the Pagan afterlife, in the title of this book it refers to the mythological landscape itself as a living, creative source that fires and sustains its people. The Summer Lands was home to the Celtic bard who tapped this wellspring of creativity through story-telling. *Timeless Tales from the Summer Lands* celebrates this tradition through the verses of Tony Cottrell and the artwork of his brother Barry. This revised and updated edition of the original 1993 *Tales from the Summer Lands* contains some additional verses and images along with detailed information about the linocut illustrations, enabling the book to serve as a catalogue for the prints.

Tony Cottrell is a poet, novelist, playwright, actor, and resident of Polruan, Cornwall. His comic novel, *Mena Dhu: A Cornish Comedy*, published by Brown Dog Books in 2020, is available on Amazon and Kindle. His novels, verse and short stories, including his *Fowey River Writings* (2021), are all available from Tony at 10 East Street, Polruan, PL23 1PB.

Barry Cottrell is an artist-printmaker, specialising in 'the driven line' - burin engraving on copper, wood and lino. He is also an author and book publisher: his most recent books of shamanic incantations, *Sounding Eternity* and *Beautiful Dream,* were published in 2021 and 2022 respectively by drivenLine, www.drivenline.uk.

9 781739 920555